The Boscombe Valley Mystery

Sherlock Holmes in Large Print

The Boscombe Valley Mystery

By: Arthur Conan Doyle

Series Editor: Craig Stephen Copland

The characters of Sherlock Holmes and Dr. Watson are in the public domain, as is the original story, The Boscombe Valley Mystery.

Published by:

Conservative Growth
1101 30th Street NW. Ste. 500
Washington, DC, 20007

.

ISBN- 10: 1535551577

ISBN-13: 978-1535551571

Dedication

Dame Jean Conan Doyle

This series of books, *The Stories of Sherlock Holmes in Large Print*, is appropriately dedicated to the memory of Jean Conan Doyle, the youngest daughter of Arthur Conan Doyle.

In addition to her years of service to the literary estate of her father and to the promotion of all things Sherlockian, Jean Conan Doyle was a highly accomplished woman in her own right. As a young woman she joined the Women's Auxiliary Air Force and served with distinction during World War II and afterward. She rose through the ranks until she was awarded the rank of Air Commandant in 1963. She was given the honor of OBE and appointed as honorary aide-de-camp to Queen Elizabeth II. Also in 1963, she was elevated to Dame Commander of the Order of the British Empire (DBE, Military Division), and became known as Dame Jean Conan Doyle.

This very impressive woman suffered from poor eyesight since she was a child and took an active interest in the welfare of the blind and those who were visually impaired. Upon her death, she donated the remaining copyrights she owned to the Royal National Institute for the Blind.

This new printing of the Canon of Sherlock Holmes stories in large print has been undertaken so that those with poor or diminishing eyesight can continue to enjoy reading and re-reading about the adventures of their beloved detective. It is following in the footsteps of Dame Jean Conan Doyle not only in its service to the visually impaired, but also in its dedication to the continuing fascination with the character of Sherlock Holmes.

Acknowledgments

All books in this series of Sherlock Holmes mysteries use the font, APHont, that was developed specifically for texts for the visually impaired by the American Printing House for the Blind. The formatting also follows the recommendations provided by this organization. If you wish to volunteer or donate to them, they can be found at www.aph.org.

Spelling and punctuation follow British practices, as did the original story.

No edition of the stories of Sherlock Holmes could ever exist were it not for the original creative brilliance of the author, Arthur Conan Doyle. To his genius in creating the character of the world's favourite detective, all Sherlockians are forever grateful.

Thanks must also go to Jon Lellenberg who for many years served as counsel to the Arthur Conan Doyle Literary Estate and who generously provided advice and direction for this series of books.

In preparing the Editor's Notes that accompany every story, I am indebted to many sources for my far-from-scholarly knowledge of The Canon. I would, however, refer readers who wish to know more about Sherlock Holmes to the following excellent works:

Christopher Redmond, *The Sherlock Holmes Handbook.*

Leslie Klinger, *The New Annotated Sherlock Holmes,*

William S. Baring Gould, *The Annotated Sherlock Holmes,* and

D. Martin Dakin, *A Sherlock Holmes Commentary*.

If you notice any errors or omissions, or you have suggestions that would make these books even better for seniors and visually impaired readers, please report them to sherlock75holmes@aol.com.

Thank you.

Craig Stephen Copland

Series Editor

The Boscombe Valley Mystery

We were seated at breakfast one morning, my wife and I, when the maid brought in a telegram. It was from Sherlock Holmes and ran in this way:

Have you a couple of days to spare? Have just been wired for from the west of England in connection with Boscombe Valley tragedy. Shall be glad if you will come with me. Air and scenery perfect. Leave Paddington by the 11:15.

"What do you say, dear?" said my wife, looking across at me. "Will you go?"

"I really don't know what to say. I have a fairly long list at present."

"Oh, Anstruther would do your work for you. You have been looking a little pale lately. I think that the change would do you good, and you are always so interested in Mr. Sherlock Holmes's cases."

"I should be ungrateful if I were not, seeing what I gained through one of them," I answered. "But if I am to go, I must pack at once, for I have only half an hour."

My experience of camp life in Afghanistan had at least had the effect of making me a prompt and ready traveller. My wants were few and simple, so that in less than the time stated I was in a cab with my valise, rattling away to Paddington Station. Sherlock Holmes was pacing up and down the platform, his tall, gaunt figure made even gaunter and taller by his long gray travelling-cloak and close-fitting cloth cap.

"It is really very good of you to come, Watson," said he. "It makes a considerable difference to me, having someone with me on whom I can thoroughly rely. Local aid is always either worthless or else biassed. If you will keep the two corner seats I shall get the tickets."

We had the carriage to ourselves save for an immense litter of papers which Holmes had brought with him. Among these he rummaged and read, with intervals of note-taking and of meditation, until we were past Reading. Then he suddenly rolled them all into a gigantic ball and tossed them up onto the rack.

"Have you heard anything of the case?" he asked.

"Not a word. I have not seen a paper for some days."

"The London press has not had very full accounts. I have just been looking through all the recent papers in order to master the particulars. It seems, from what I gather, to be one of those simple cases which are so extremely difficult."

"That sounds a little paradoxical."

"But it is profoundly true. Singularity is almost invariably a clew. The more featureless and commonplace a crime is, the more difficult it is to bring it home. In this case, however, they have established a very serious case against the son of the murdered man."

"It is a murder, then?"

"Well, it is conjectured to be so. I shall take

nothing for granted until I have the opportunity of looking personally into it. I will explain the state of things to you, as far as I have been able to understand it, in a very few words.

"Boscombe Valley is a country district not very far from Ross, in Herefordshire. The largest landed proprietor in that part is a Mr. John Turner, who made his money in Australia and returned some years ago to the old country. One of the farms which he held, that of Hatherley, was let to Mr. Charles McCarthy, who was also an ex-Australian. The men had known each other in the colonies, so that it was not unnatural that when they came to settle down they should do so as near each other as possible. Turner was apparently the richer man, so McCarthy became his tenant but still remained, it seems, upon terms of perfect equality, as they were frequently together. McCarthy had one son, a lad of eighteen, and Turner had an only daughter of the same age, but neither of them had wives living. They appear to have avoided the society of the neighboring English families and to have led retired lives, though both the McCarthys were fond of sport and were frequently seen at the race-meetings of the neighborhood. McCarthy kept two servants--a man and a girl. Turner had a considerable household, some half-dozen at the least. That is as much as I have been able to gather about the families. Now for the facts.

"On June 3rd, that is, on Monday last, McCarthy left his house at Hatherley about three in the afternoon and walked down to the Boscombe Pool, which is a small lake formed by the spreading out of the stream which runs down the Boscombe Valley. He had been out with his serving-man in the morning at Ross, and he had told the man that he must hurry, as he had an appointment of importance to keep at three. From that appointment he never came back alive.

"From Hatherley Farm-house to the Boscombe Pool is a quarter of a mile, and two people saw him as he passed over this ground. One was an old woman, whose name is not mentioned, and the other was William Crowder, a game-keeper in the employ of Mr. Turner. Both these witnesses depose that Mr. McCarthy was walking alone. The game-keeper adds that within a few minutes of his seeing Mr. McCarthy pass he had seen his son, Mr. James McCarthy, going the same way with a gun under his arm. To the best of his belief, the father was actually in sight at the time, and the son was following him. He thought no more of the matter until he heard in the evening of the tragedy that had occurred.

"The two McCarthys were seen after the time when William Crowder, the game-keeper, lost sight of them. The Boscombe Pool is thickly wooded round, with just a fringe of grass and of reeds round the edge. A girl of fourteen, Patience Moran, who is the daughter of the lodge-keeper of the Boscombe Valley estate, was in one of the woods picking flowers. She states that while she was there she saw, at the border of the wood and close by the lake, Mr. McCarthy and his son, and that they appeared to be having a violent quarrel. She heard Mr. McCarthy the elder using very strong language to his son, and she saw the latter raise up his hand as if to strike his father. She was so frightened by their violence that she ran away and told her mother when she reached home that she had left the two McCarthys quarrelling near Boscombe Pool, and that she was afraid that they were going to fight. She had hardly said the words when young Mr. McCarthy came running up to the lodge to say that he had found his father dead in the wood, and to ask for the help of the lodge-keeper. He was much excited, without either his gun or his hat, and his right hand and sleeve were observed to be stained with fresh blood. On following him they found the dead body stretched out upon the grass beside the pool. The head had been beaten in by repeated blows of some heavy and blunt weapon. The injuries were such as might very well have been inflicted by the butt-end of his son's gun, which was found lying on the grass within a few paces of the body. Under these circumstances the young man was instantly arrested, and a verdict of 'wilful murder' having been returned at the inquest on Tuesday, he was on Wednesday brought before the magistrates at Ross, who have referred the case to the next Assizes. Those are the main facts of the case as they came out before the coroner and the police-court."

"I could hardly imagine a more damning case," I remarked. "If ever circumstantial evidence pointed to a criminal it does so here."

"Circumstantial evidence is a very tricky thing," answered Holmes thoughtfully. "It may seem to point very straight to one thing, but if you shift your own point of view a little, you may find it pointing in an equally uncompromising manner to something entirely different. It must be confessed, however, that the case looks exceedingly grave against the young man, and it is very possible that he is indeed the culprit.

There are several people in the neighborhood, however, and among them Miss Turner, the daughter of the neighboring landowner, who believe in his innocence, and who have retained Lestrade, whom you may recollect in connection with 'A Study in Scarlet', to work out the case in his interest. Lestrade, being rather puzzled, has referred the case to me, and hence it is that two middle-aged gentlemen are flying westward at fifty miles an hour instead of quietly digesting their breakfasts at home."

"I am afraid," said I, "that the facts are so obvious that you will find little credit to be gained out of this case."

"There is nothing more deceptive than an obvious fact," he answered, laughing. "Besides, we may chance to hit upon some other obvious facts which may have been by no means obvious to Mr.

Lestrade. You know me too well to think that I am boasting when I say that I shall either confirm or destroy his theory by means which he is quite incapable of employing, or even of understanding. To take the first example to hand, I very clearly perceive that in your bedroom the window is upon the right-hand side, and yet I question whether Mr. Lestrade would have noted even so self-evident a thing as that."

"How on earth--"

"My dear fellow, I know you well. I know the military neatness which characterizes you. You shave every morning, and in this season you shave by the sunlight; but since your shaving is less and less complete as we get farther back on the left side, until it becomes positively slovenly as we get round the angle of the jaw, it is surely very clear that that side is less illuminated than the other. I could not imagine a man of your habits looking at himself in an equal light and being satisfied with such a result. I only quote this as a trivial example of observation and inference. Therein lies my metier, and it is just possible that it may be of some service in the investigation which lies before us. There are one or two minor points which were brought out in the inquest, and which are worth considering."

"What are they?"

"It appears that his arrest did not take place at once, but after the return to Hatherley Farm. On the inspector of constabulary informing him that he was a prisoner, he remarked that he was not surprised to hear it, and that it was no more than his deserts. This observation of his had the natural effect of removing any traces of doubt which might have remained in the minds of the coroner's jury."

"It was a confession," I ejaculated.

"No, for it was followed by a protestation of innocence."

"Coming on the top of such a damning series of events, it was at least a most suspicious remark."

"On the contrary," said Holmes, "it is the brightest rift which I can at present see in the clouds. However innocent he might be, he could not be such an absolute imbecile as not to see that the circumstances were very black against him. Had he appeared surprised at his own arrest, or feigned indignation at it, I should have looked upon it as highly suspicious, because such surprise or anger would not be natural under the circumstances, and yet might appear to be the best policy to a scheming man. His frank acceptance of the situation marks him as either an innocent man, or else as a man of considerable self-restraint and firmness. As to his remark about his deserts, it was also not unnatural if you consider that he stood beside the dead body of his father, and that there is no doubt that he had that very day so far forgotten his filial duty as to bandy words with him, and even, according to the little girl whose evidence is so important, to raise his hand as if to strike him. The self-reproach and contrition which are displayed in his remark appear to me to be the signs of a healthy mind rather than of a guilty on."

I shook my head. "Many men have been hanged on far slighter evidence," I remarked.

"So they have. And many men have been wrongfully hanged."

"What is the young man's own account of the matter?"

"It is, I am afraid, not very encouraging to his supporters, though there are one or two points in it which are suggestive. You will find it here, and may read it for yourself."

He picked out from his bundle a copy of the local Herefordshire paper, and having turned down the sheet he pointed out the paragraph in which the unfortunate young man had given his own statement of what had occurred. I settled myself down in the corner of the carriage and read it very carefully. It ran in this way:

Mr. James McCarthy, the only son of the deceased, was then called and gave evidence as follows: "I had been away from home for three days at Bristol, and had only just returned upon the morning of last Monday, the 3d. My father was absent from home at the time of my arrival, and I was informed by the maid that he had driven over to Ross with John Cobb, the groom. Shortly after my return I heard the wheels of his trap in the yard, and, looking out of my window, I saw him get out and walk rapidly out of the yard, though I was not aware in which direction he was going. I then took my gun and strolled out in the direction of the Boscombe Pool, with the intention of visiting the rabbit warren which is upon the other side. On my way I saw William Crowder, the game-keeper, as he had stated in his evidence; but he is mistaken in thinking that I was following my father. I had no idea that he was in front of me. When about a hundred yards from the pool I heard a cry of 'Cooee!' which was a usual signal between my father and myself. I then hurried forward, and found him standing by the pool. He appeared to be much surprised at seeing me and asked me rather roughly what I was doing there. A conversation ensued which led to high words and almost to blows, for my father was a man of a very violent temper. Seeing that his passion was becoming ungovernable, I left him and returned towards Hatherley Farm. I had not gone more than 150 yards, however, when I heard a hideous outcry behind me, which caused me to run back again. I found my father expiring upon the ground, with his head terribly injured. I dropped my gun and held him in my arms, but he almost instantly expired. I knelt beside him for some minutes, and then made my way to Mr. Turner's lodge-keeper, his house being the nearest, to ask for assistance. I saw no one near my father when I returned, and I have no idea how he came by his injuries. He was not a popular man, being somewhat cold and forbidding in his manners, but he had, as far as I know, no active enemies. I know nothing further of the matter."

"The Coroner: 'Did your father make any statement to you before he died?'

"Witness: 'He mumbled a few words, but I could only catch some allusion to a rat.'

"The Coroner: 'What did you understand by that?'

"Witness: 'It conveyed no meaning to me. I thought that he was delirious.'

"The Coroner: 'What was the point upon which you and your father had this final quarrel?'

"Witness: 'I should prefer not to answer.'

"The Coroner: 'I am afraid that I must press it.'

"Witness: 'It is really impossible for me to tell you. I can assure you that it has nothing to do with the sad tragedy which followed.'

"The Coroner: 'That is for the court to decide. I need not point out to you that your refusal to answer will prejudice your case considerably in any future proceedings which may arise'

"Witness: 'I must still refuse.'

"The Coroner: 'I understand that the cry of "Cooee" was a common signal between you and your father?'

"Witness: 'It was.'

"The Coroner: 'How was it, then, that he uttered it before he saw you, and before he even knew that you had returned from Bristol?'

"Witness (with considerable confusion): 'I do not know.'

"A Juryman: 'Did you see nothing which aroused

your suspicions when you returned on hearing the cry and found your father fatally injured?'

"Witness: 'Nothing definite.'

"The Coroner: 'What do you mean?'

"Witness: 'I was so disturbed and excited as I rushed out into the open, that I could think of nothing except of my father. Yet I have a vague impression that as I ran forward something lay upon the ground to the left of me. It seemed to me to be something gray in color, a coat of some sort, or a plaid perhaps. When I rose from my father I looked round for it, but it was gone.'

"'Do you mean that it disappeared before you went for help?'

"'Yes, it was gone.'

"'You cannot say what it was?'

"'No, I had a feeling something was there.'

"'How far from the body?'

"'A dozen yards or so.'

"'And how far from the edge of the wood?'

"'About the same.'

"'Then if it was removed it was while you were within a dozen yards of it?'

"'Yes, but with my back towards it.'

"This concluded the examination of the witness."

"I see," said I as I glanced down the column, "that the coroner in his concluding remarks was rather severe upon young McCarthy. He calls attention, and with reason, to the discrepancy about his father having signalled to him before seeing him also to his refusal to give details of his conversation with his father, and his singular account of his father's dying words. They are all, as he remarks, very much against the son."

Holmes laughed softly to himself and stretched himself out upon the cushioned seat. "Both you and the coroner have been at some pains," said he, "to single out the very strongest points in the young man's favor. Don't you see that you alternately give him credit for having too much imagination and too little? Too little, if he could not invent a cause of quarrel which would give him the sympathy of the jury; too much, if he evolved from his own inner consciousness anything so outre as a dying reference to a rat, and the incident of the vanishing cloth. No, sir, I shall approach this case from the point of view that what this young man says is true, and we shall see whither that hypothesis will lead us. And now here is my pocket Petrarch, and not another word shall I say of this case until we are on the scene of action. We lunch at Swindon, and I see that we shall be there in twenty minutes."

It was nearly four o'clock when we at last, after passing through the beautiful Stroud Valley, and over the broad gleaming Severn, found ourselves at the pretty little country-town of Ross. A lean, ferret-like man, furtive and sly-looking, was waiting for us upon the platform. In spite of the light brown dustcoat and leather-leggings which he wore in deference to his rustic surroundings, I had no difficulty in recognizing Lestrade, of Scotland Yard. With him we drove to the Hereford Arms where a room had already been engaged for us.

"I have ordered a carriage," said Lestrade as we sat over a cup of tea. "I knew your energetic nature, and that you would not be happy until you had been on the scene of the crime."

"It was very nice and complimentary of you," Holmes answered. "It is entirely a question of barometric pressure."

Lestrade looked startled. "I do not quite follow," he said.

"How is the glass? Twenty-nine, I see. No wind, and not a cloud in the sky. I have a caseful of cigarettes here which need smoking, and the sofa is very much superior to the usual country hotel abomination. I do not think that it is probable that I shall use the carriage to-night."

Lestrade laughed indulgently. "You have, no doubt, already formed your conclusions from the newspapers," he said. "The case is as plain as a pikestaff, and the more one goes into it the plainer it becomes. Still, of course, one can't refuse a lady, and such a very positive one, too. She has heard of you, and would have your opinion, though I repeatedly told her that there was nothing which you could do which I had not already done. Why, bless my soul! here is her carriage at the door."

He had hardly spoken before there rushed into the room one of the most lovely young women that I have ever seen in my life. Her violet eyes shining, her lips parted, a pink flush upon her cheeks, all thought of her natural reserve lost in her overpowering excitement and concern.

"Oh, Mr. Sherlock Holmes!" she cried, glancing from one to the other of us, and finally, with a woman's quick intuition, fastening upon my companion, "I am so glad that you have come. I have driven down to tell you so. I know that James didn't do it. I know it, and I want you to start upon your work knowing it, too. Never let yourself doubt upon that point. We have known each other since we were little children, and I know his faults as no one else does; but he is too tenderhearted to hurt a fly. Such a charge is absurd to anyone who really knows him."

"I hope we may clear him, Miss Turner," said Sherlock Holmes. "You may rely upon my doing all that I can."

"But you have read the evidence. You have formed some conclusion? Do you not see some loophole, some flaw? Do you not yourself think that he is innocent?"

"I think that it is very probable."

"There, now!" she cried, throwing back her head and looking defiantly at Lestrade. "You hear! He gives me hopes."

Lestrade shrugged his shoulders. "I am afraid that my colleague has been a little quick in forming his conclusions," he said.

"But he is right. Oh! I know that he is right. James never did it. And about his quarrel with his father, I am sure that the reason why he would not speak about it to the coroner was because I was concerned in it."

"In what way?" asked Holmes.

"It is no time for me to hide anything. James and his father had many disagreements about me. Mr. McCarthy was very anxious that there should be a marriage between us. James and I have always loved each other as brother and sister; but of course he is young and has seen very little of life yet, and--and--well, he naturally did not wish to do anything like that yet. So there were quarrels, and this, I am sure, was one of them."

"And your father?" asked Holmes. "Was he in favor of such a union?"

"No, he was averse to it also. No one but Mr. McCarthy was in favor of it." A quick blush passed over her fresh young face as Holmes shot one of his keen, questioning glances at her.

"Thank you for this information," said he. "May I see your father if I call to-morrow?"

"I am afraid the doctor won't allow it."

"The doctor?"

"Yes, have you not heard? Poor father has never been strong for years back, but this has broken him down completely. He has taken to his bed, and Dr. Willows says that he is a wreck and that his nervous system is shattered. Mr. McCarthy was the only man alive who had known dad in the old days in Victoria."

"Ha! In Victoria! That is important."

"Yes, at the mines."

"Quite so; at the gold-mines, where, as I understand, Mr. Turner made his money."

"Yes, certainly."

"Thank you, Miss Turner. You have been of material assistance to me."

"You will tell me if you have any news to-morrow. No doubt you will go to the prison to see James. Oh, if you do, Mr. Holmes, do tell him that I know him to be innocent."

"I will, Miss Turner."

"I must go home now, for dad is very ill, and he misses me so if I leave him. Good-bye, and God help you in your undertaking." She hurried from the room as impulsively as she had entered, and we heard the wheels of her carriage rattle off down the street.

"I am ashamed of you, Holmes," said Lestrade with dignity after a few minutes' silence. "Why should you raise up hopes which you are bound to disappoint? I am not over-tender of heart, but I call it cruel."

"I think that I see my way to clearing James McCarthy," said Holmes. "Have you an order to see him in prison?"

"Yes, but only for you and me."

"Then I shall reconsider my resolution about going out. We have still time to take a train to Hereford and see him to-night?"

"Ample."

"Then let us do so. Watson, I fear that you will find it very slow, but I shall only be away a couple of hours."

I walked down to the station with them, and then wandered through the streets of the little town, finally returning to the hotel, where I lay upon the sofa and tried to interest myself in a yellow-backed novel. The puny plot of the story was so thin, however, when compared to the deep mystery through which we were groping, and I found my attention wander so continually from the action to the fact, that I at last flung it across the room and gave myself up entirely to a consideration of the events of the day. Supposing that this unhappy young man's story were absolutely true, then what hellish thing, what absolutely unforeseen and extraordinary calamity could have occurred between the time when he parted from his father, and the moment when drawn back by his screams, he rushed into the glade? It was something terrible and deadly. What could it be? Might not the nature of the injuries reveal something to my medical instincts? I rang the bell and called for the weekly county paper, which contained a verbatim account of the inquest. In the surgeon's deposition it was stated that the posterior third of the left parietal bone and the left half of the occipital bone hail been shattered by a heavy blow from a blunt weapon. I marked the spot upon my own head. Clearly such a blow must have been struck from behind. That was to some extent in favor of the accused, as when seen quarrelling he was face to face with his father. Still, it did not go for very much, for the older man might have turned his back before the blow fell. Still, it might be worth while to call Holmes's attention to it. Then there was the peculiar dying reference to a rat. What could that mean? It could not be delirium. A man dying from a sudden blow does not commonly become delirious. No, it was more likely to be an attempt to explain how he met his fate. But what could it indicate? I cudgelled my brains to find some possible explanation. And then the incident of the gray cloth seen by young McCarthy. If that were true the murderer must have dropped some part of his dress, presumably his overcoat, in his flight, and must have had the hardihood to return and to carry it away at the instant when the son was kneeling with his back turned not a dozen paces off. What a tissue of mysteries and improbabilities the whole thing was! I did not wonder at Lestrade's opinion, and yet I had so much faith in Sherlock Holmes's insight that I could not lose hope as long as every fresh fact seemed to strengthen his conviction of young McCarthy's innocence.

It was late before Sherlock Holmes returned. He came back alone, for Lestrade was staying in lodgings in the town.

"The glass still keeps very high," he remarked as he sat down. "It is of importance that it should not rain before we are able to go over the ground. On the other hand, a man should be at his very best and keenest for such nice work as that, and I did not wish to do it when fagged by a long journey. I have seen young McCarthy."

"And what did you learn from him?"

"Nothing."

"Could he throw no light?"

"None at all. I was inclined to think at one time that he knew who had done it and was screening him or her, but I am convinced now that he is as puzzled as everyone else. He is not a very quick-witted youth, though comely to look at and, I should think, sound at heart."

"I cannot admire his taste," I remarked, "if it is indeed a fact that he was averse to a marriage with so charming a young lady as this Miss Turner."

"Ah, thereby hangs a rather painful tale. This fellow is madly, insanely, in love with her, but some two years ago, when he was only a lad, and before he really knew her, for she had been away five years at a boarding-school, what does the idiot do but get into the clutches of a barmaid in Bristol and marry her at a registry office? No one knows a word of the matter, but you can imagine how maddening it must be to him to be upbraided for not doing what he would give his very eyes to do, but what he knows to be absolutely impossible. It was sheer frenzy of this sort which made him throw his hands up into the air when his father, at their last interview, was goading him on to propose to Miss Turner. On the other hand, he had no means of supporting himself, and his father, who was by all accounts a very hard man, would have thrown him over utterly had he known the truth. It was with his barmaid wife that he had spent the last three days in Bristol, and his father did not know where he was. Mark that point. It is of importance. Good has come out of evil, however, for the barmaid, finding from the papers that he is in serious trouble and likely to be hanged, has thrown him over utterly and has written to him to say that she has a husband already in the Bermuda Dockyard, so that there is really no tie between them. I think that that bit of news has consoled young McCarthy for all that he has suffered."

"But if he is innocent, who has done it?"

"Ah! who? I would call your attention very particularly to two points. One is that the murdered man had an appointment with someone at the pool, and that the someone could not have been his son, for his son was away, and he did not know when he would return. The second is that the murdered man was heard to cry 'Cooee!' before he knew that his son had returned. Those are the crucial points upon which the case depends. And now let us talk about George Meredith, if you please, and we shall leave all minor matters until to-morrow."

There was no rain, as Holmes had foretold, and the morning broke bright and cloudless. At nine o'clock Lestrade called for us with the carriage, and we set off for Hatherley Farm and the Boscombe Pool.

"There is serious news this morning," Lestrade observed. "It is said that Mr. Turner, of the Hall, is so ill that his life is despaired of."

"An elderly man, I presume?" said Holmes.

"About sixty; but his constitution has been shattered by his life abroad, and he has been in failing health for some time. This business has had a very bad effect upon him. He was an old friend of McCarthy's, and, I may add, a great benefactor to him, for I have learned that he gave him Hatherley Farm rent free."

"Indeed! That is interesting," said Holmes.

"Oh, yes! In a hundred other ways he has helped him. Everybody about here speaks of his kindness to him."

"Really! Does it not strike you as a little singular that this McCarthy, who appears to have had little of his own, and to have been under such obligations to Turner, should still talk of marrying his son to Turner's daughter, who is, presumably, heiress to the estate, and that in such a very cocksure manner, as if it were merely a case of a proposal and all else would follow? It is the more strange, since we know that Turner himself was averse to the idea. The daughter told us as much. Do you not deduce something from that?"

"We have got to the deductions and the inferences," said Lestrade, winking at me. "I find it hard enough to tackle facts, Holmes, without flying away after theories and fancies."

"You are right," said Holmes demurely; "you do find it very hard to tackle the facts."

"Anyhow, I have grasped one fact which you

seem to find it difficult to get hold of," replied Lestrade with some warmth.

"And that is--"

"That McCarthy senior met his death from McCarthy junior and that all theories to the contrary are the merest moonshine."

"Well, moonshine is a brighter thing than fog," said Holmes, laughing. "But I am very much mistaken if this is not Hatherley Farm upon the left."

"Yes, that is it." It was a widespread, comfortable-looking building, two-storied, slate-roofed, with great yellow blotches of lichen upon the gray walls. The drawn blinds and the smokeless chimneys, however, gave it a stricken look, as though the weight of this horror still lay heavy upon it. We called at the door, when the maid, at Holmes's request, showed us the boots which her master wore at the time of his death, and also a pair of the son's, though not the pair which he had then had. Having measured these very carefully from seven or eight different points, Holmes desired to be led to the court-yard, from which we all followed the winding track which led to Boscombe Pool.

Sherlock Holmes was transformed when he was hot upon such a scent as this. Men who had only known the quiet thinker and logician of Baker Street would have failed to recognize him. His face flushed and darkened. His brows were drawn into two hard black lines, while his eyes shone out from beneath them with a steely glitter. His face was bent downward, his shoulders bowed, his lips compressed, and the veins stood out like whipcord in his long, sinewy neck. His nostrils seemed to dilate with a purely animal lust for the chase, and his mind was so absolutely concentrated upon the matter before him that a question or remark fell unheeded upon his ears, or, at the most, only provoked a quick, impatient snarl in reply. Swiftly and silently he made his way along the track which ran through the meadows, and so by way of the woods to the Boscombe Pool. It was damp, marshy ground, as is all that district, and there were marks of many feet, both upon the path and amid the short grass which bounded it on either side. Sometimes Holmes would hurry on, sometimes stop dead, and once he made quite a little detour into the meadow. Lestrade and I walked behind him, the detective indifferent and contemptuous, while I watched my friend with the interest which sprang from the conviction that every one of his actions was directed towards a definite end.

The Boscombe Pool, which is a little reed-girt sheet of water some fifty yards across, is situated at the boundary between the Hatherley Farm and the private park of the wealthy Mr. Turner. Above the woods which lined it upon the farther side we could see the red, jutting pinnacles which marked the site of the rich landowner's dwelling. On the Hatherley side of the pool the woods grew very thick, and there was a narrow belt of sodden grass twenty paces across between the edge of the trees land the reeds which lined the lake. Lestrade showed us the exact spot at which the body had been found, and, indeed, so moist was the ground, that I could plainly see the traces which had been left by the fall of the stricken man. To Holmes, as I could see by his eager face and peering eyes, very many other things were to be read upon the trampled grass. He ran round, like a dog who is picking up a scent, and then turned upon my companion.

"What did you go into the pool for?" he asked.

"I fished about with a rake. I thought there might be some weapon or other trace. But how on earth--"

"Oh, tut, tut! I have no time! That left foot of yours with its inward twist is all over the place. A mole could trace it, and there it vanishes among the reeds. Oh, how simple it would all have been had I been here before they came like a herd of buffalo and wallowed all over it. Here is where the party with the lodge-keeper came, and they have covered all tracks for six or eight feet round the body. But here are three separate tracks of the same feet." He drew out a lens and lay down upon his waterproof to have a better view, talking all the time rather to himself than to us. "These are young McCarthy's feet. Twice he was walking, and once he ran swiftly, so that the soles are deeply marked and the heels hardly visible. That bears out his story. He ran when he saw his father on the ground. Then here are the father's feet as he paced up and down. What is this, then? It is the butt-end of the gun as the son stood listening. And this? Ha, ha! What have we here? Tiptoes! tiptoes! Square, too, quite unusual boots! They come, they go, they come again--of course that was for the cloak. Now where did they come from?" He ran up and down, sometimes losing, sometimes finding the track until we were well within the edge of the wood and under the shadow of a great beech, the largest tree in the neighborhood. Holmes traced his way to the farther side of this and lay down once more upon his face with a little cry of satisfaction. For a long time he remained there, turning over the leaves and dried sticks, gathering up what seemed to me to be dust into an envelope and examining with his lens not only the ground but even the bark of the tree as far as he could reach. A jagged stone was lying among the moss, and this also he carefully examined and retained. Then he followed a pathway through the wood until he came to the highroad, where all traces were lost.

"It has been a case of considerable interest," he remarked, returning to his natural manner. "I fancy that this gray house on the right must be the lodge. I think that I will go in and have a word with Moran, and perhaps write a little note. Having done that, we may drive back to our luncheon. You may walk to the cab, and I shall be with you presently."

It was about ten minutes before we regained our cab and drove back into Ross, Holmes still carrying with him the stone which he had picked up in the wood.

"This may interest you, Lestrade," he remarked, holding it out. "The murder was done with it."

"I see no marks."

"There are none."

"How do you know, then?"

"The grass was growing under it. It had only lain there a few days. There was no sign of a place whence it had been taken. It corresponds with the injuries. There is no sign of any other weapon."

"And the murderer?"

"Is a tall man, left-handed, limps with the right leg, wears thick-soled shooting-boots and a gray cloak, smokes Indian cigars, uses a cigar-holder, and carries a blunt pen-knife in his pocket. There are several other indications, but these may be enough to aid us in our search."

Lestrade laughed. "I am afraid that I am still a sceptic," he said. "Theories are all very well, but we have to deal with a hard-headed British jury."

"Nous verrons," answered Holmes calmly. "You work your own method, and I shall work mine. I shall be busy this afternoon, and shall probably return to London by the evening train."

"And leave your case unfinished?"

"No, finished."

"But the mystery?"

"It is solved."

"Who was the criminal, then?"

"The gentleman I describe."

"But who is he?"

"Surely it would not be difficult to find out. This is not such a populous neighborhood."

Lestrade shrugged his shoulders. "I am a practical man," he said, "and I really cannot undertake to go about the country looking for a left-handed gentleman with a game leg. I should become the laughing-stock of Scotland Yard."

"All right," said Holmes quietly. "I have given you the chance. Here are your lodgings. Good-bye. I shall drop you a line before I leave."

Having left Lestrade at his rooms, we drove to our hotel, where we found lunch upon the table. Holmes was silent and buried in thought with a pained expression upon his face, as one who finds himself in a perplexing position.

"Look here, Watson," he said when the cloth was

cleared "just sit down in this chair and let me preach to you for a little. I don't know quite what to do, and I should value your advice. Light a cigar and let me expound."

"Pray do so."

"Well, now, in considering this case there are two points about young McCarthy's narrative which struck us both instantly, although they impressed me in his favor and you against him. One was the fact that his father should, according to his account, cry 'Cooee!' before seeing him. The other was his singular dying reference to a rat. He mumbled several words, you understand, but that was all that caught the son's ear. Now from this double point our research must commence, and we will begin it by presuming that what the lad says is absolutely true."

"What of this 'Cooee!' then?"

"Well, obviously it could not have been meant for the son. The son, as far as he knew, was in Bristol. It was mere chance that he was within earshot. The 'Cooee!' was meant to attract the attention of whoever it was that he had the appointment with. But 'Cooee' is a distinctly Australian cry, and one which is used between Australians. There is a strong presumption that the person whom McCarthy expected to meet him at Boscombe Pool was someone who had been in Australia."

"What of the rat, then?"

Sherlock Holmes took a folded paper from his pocket and flattened it out on the table. "This is a map of the Colony of Victoria," he said. "I wired to Bristol for it last night." He put his hand over part of the map. "What do you read?"

"*Arat*," I read.

"And now?" He raised his hand.

"*Ballarat*."

"Quite so. That was the word the man uttered, and of which his son only caught the last two syllables. He was trying to utter the name of his murderer. So and so, of Ballarat."

"It is wonderful!" I exclaimed.

"It is obvious. And now, you see, I had narrowed the field down considerably. The possession of a gray garment was a third point which, granting the son's statement to be correct, was a certainty. We have come now out of mere vagueness to the definite conception of an Australian from Ballarat with a gray cloak."

"Certainly."

"And one who was at home in the district, for the pool can only be approached by the farm or by the estate, where strangers could hardly wander."

"Quite so."

"Then comes our expedition of to-day. By an examination of the ground I gained the trifling details which I gave to that imbecile Lestrade, as to the personality of the criminal."

"But how did you gain them?"

"You know my method. It is founded upon the observation of trifles."

"His height I know that you might roughly judge from the length of his stride. His boots, too, might be told from their traces."

"Yes, they were peculiar boots."

"But his lameness?"

"The impression of his right foot was always less distinct than his left. He put less weight upon it.

Why? Because he limped--he was lame."

"But his left-handedness."

"You were yourself struck by the nature of the injury as recorded by the surgeon at the inquest. The blow was struck from immediately behind, and yet was upon the left side. Now, how can that be unless it were by a left-handed man? He had stood behind that tree during the interview between the father and son. He had even smoked there. I found the ash of a cigar, which my special knowledge of tobacco ashes enables me to pronounce as an Indian cigar. I have, as you know, devoted some attention to this, and written a little monograph on the ashes of 140 different varieties of pipe, cigar, and cigarette tobacco. Having found the ash, I then looked round and discovered the stump among the moss where he had tossed it. It was an Indian cigar, of the variety which are rolled in Rotterdam."

"And the cigar-holder?"

"I could see that the end had not been in his mouth. Therefore he used a holder. The tip had been cut off, not bitten off, but the cut was not a clean one, so I deduced a blunt pen-knife."

"Holmes," I said, "you have drawn a net round this man from which he cannot escape, and you have saved an innocent human life as truly as if you had cut the cord which was hanging him. I see the direction in which all this points. The culprit is--"

"Mr. John Turner," cried the hotel waiter, opening the door of our sitting-room, and ushering in a visitor.

The man who entered was a strange and impressive figure. His slow, limping step and bowed shoulders gave the appearance of decrepitude, and yet his hard, deep-lined, craggy features, and his enormous limbs showed that he was possessed of unusual strength of body and of character. His tangled beard, grizzled hair, and outstanding, drooping eyebrows combined to give an air of dignity and power to his appearance, but his face was of an ashen white, while his lips and the corners of his nostrils were tinged with a shade of blue. It was clear to me at a glance that he was in the grip of some deadly and chronic disease.

"Pray sit down on the sofa," said Holmes gently. "You had my note?"

"Yes, the lodge-keeper brought it up. You said that you wished to see me here to avoid scandal."

"I thought people would talk if I went to the Hall."

"And why did you wish to see me?" He looked across at my companion with despair in his weary eyes, as though his question was already answered.

"Yes," said Holmes, answering the look rather than the words. "It is so. I know all about McCarthy."

The old man sank his face in his hands. "God help me!" he cried. "But I would not have let the young man come to harm. I give you my word that I would have spoken out if it went against him at the Assizes."

"I am glad to hear you say so," said Holmes gravely.

"I would have spoken now had it not been for my dear girl. It would break her heart--it will break her heart when she hears that I am arrested."

"It may not come to that," said Holmes.

"What?"

"I am no official agent. I understand that it was your daughter who required my presence here, and I am acting in her interests. Young McCarthy must be got off, however."

"I am a dying man," said old Turner. "I have had diabetes for years. My doctor says it is a question whether I shall live a month. Yet I would rather die under my own roof than in a jail."

Holmes rose and sat down at the table with his pen in his hand and a bundle of paper before him. "Just tell us the truth," he said. "I shall jot down the facts. You will sign it, and Watson here can witness it. Then I could produce your confession at the last extremity to save young

McCarthy. I promise you that I shall not use it unless it is absolutely needed."

"It's as well," said the old man; "it's a question whether I shall live to the Assizes, so it matters little to me, but I should wish to spare Alice the shock. And now I will make the thing clear to you; it has been a long time in the acting, but will not take me long to tell.

"You didn't know this dead man, McCarthy. He was a devil incarnate. I tell you that. God keep you out of the clutches of such a man as he. His grip has been upon me these twenty years, and he has blasted my life. I'll tell you first how I came to be in his power.

"It was in the early '60's at the diggings. I was a young chap then, hot-blooded and reckless, ready to turn my hand at anything; I got among bad companions, took to drink, had no luck with my claim, took to the bush, and in a word became what you would call over here a highway robber. There were six of us, and we had a wild, free life of it, sticking up a station from time to time, or stopping the wagons on the road to the diggings. Black Jack of Ballarat was the name I went under, and our party is still remembered in the colony as the Ballarat Gang.

"One day a gold convoy came down from Ballarat to Melbourne, and we lay in wait for it and attacked it. There were six troopers and six of us, so it was a close thing, but we emptied four of their saddles at the first volley. Three of our boys were killed, however, before we got the swag. I put my pistol to the head of the wagon-driver, who was this very man McCarthy. I wish to the Lord that I had shot him then, but I spared him, though I saw his wicked little eyes fixed on my face, as though to remember every feature. We got away with the gold, became wealthy men, and made our way over to England without being suspected. There I parted from my old pals and determined to settle down to a quiet and respectable life. I bought this estate, which chanced to be in the market, and I set myself to do a little good with my money, to make up for the way in which I had earned it. I married, too, and though my wife died young she left me my dear little Alice. Even when she was just a baby her wee hand seemed to lead me down the right path as nothing else had ever done. In a word, I turned over a new leaf and did my best to make up for the past. All was going well when McCarthy laid his grip upon me.

"I had gone up to town about an investment, and I met him in Regent Street with hardly a coat to his back or a boot to his foot.

"'Here we are, Jack,' says he, touching me on the arm; 'we'll be as good as a family to you. There's two of us, me and my son, and you can have the keeping of us. If you don't--it's a fine, law-abiding country is England, and there's always a policeman within hail.'

"Well, down they came to the west country, there was no shaking them off, and there they have lived rent free on my best land ever since. There was no rest for me, no peace, no forgetfulness; turn where I would, there was his cunning, grinning face at my elbow. It grew worse as Alice grew up, for he soon saw I was more afraid of her knowing my past than of the police. Whatever he wanted he must have, and whatever it was I gave him without question, land, money, houses, until at last he asked a thing which I could not give. He asked for Alice.

"His son, you see, had grown up, and so had my girl, and as I was known to be in weak health, it seemed a fine stroke to him that his lad should step into the whole property. But there I was firm. I would not have his cursed stock mixed with mine; not that I had any dislike to the lad, but his blood was in him, and that was enough. I stood firm. McCarthy threatened. I braved him to do his worst. We were to meet at the pool midway between our houses to talk it over.

"When we went down there I found him talking with his son, so smoked a cigar and waited behind a tree until he should be alone. But as I listened to his talk all that was black and bitter in me seemed to come uppermost. He was urging his son to marry my daughter with as little regard for what she might think as if she were a slut from off the streets. It drove me mad to think that I and all that I held most dear should be in the power of such a man as this. Could I not snap the bond? I was already a dying and a desperate man. Though clear of mind and fairly strong of limb, I knew that my own fate was sealed. But my memory and my girl! Both could be saved if I could but silence that foul tongue. I did it, Mr. Holmes. I would do it again. Deeply as I have sinned, I have led a life of martyrdom to atone for it. But that my girl should be entangled in the same meshes which held me was more than I could suffer. I struck him down with no more compunction than if he had been some foul and venomous beast. His cry brought back his son; but I had gained the cover of the wood, though I was forced to go back to fetch the cloak which I had dropped in my flight. That is the true story, gentlemen, of all that occurred."

"Well, it is not for me to judge you," said Holmes as the old man signed the statement which had been drawn out. "I pray that we may never be exposed to such a temptation."

"I pray not, sir. And what do you intend to do?"

"In view of your health, nothing. You are yourself aware that you will soon have to answer for your deed at a higher court than the Assizes. I will keep your confession, and if McCarthy is condemned I shall be forced to use it. If not, it shall never be seen by mortal eye; and your secret, whether you be alive or dead, shall be safe with us."

"Farewell, then," said the old man solemnly. "Your own deathbeds, when they come, will be the easier for the thought of the peace which you have given to mine." Tottering and shaking in all his giant frame, he stumbled slowly from the room.

"God help us!" said Holmes after a long silence. "Why does fate play such tricks with poor, helpless worms? I never hear of such a case as this that I do not think of Baxter's words, and say, 'There, but for the grace of God, goes Sherlock Holmes.'"

James McCarthy was acquitted at the Assizes on the strength of a number of objections which had been drawn out by Holmes and submitted to the defending counsel. Old Turner lived for seven months after our interview, but he is now dead; and there is every prospect that the son and daughter may come to live happily together in ignorance of the black cloud which rests upon their past.

About the Author
Arthur Conan Doyle

Arthur Conan Doyle was born on May 22, 1859, in Edinburgh, Scotland, the second of Charles and Mary Doyle's seven children. His mother, a well-educated woman and gifted storyteller, introduced her son to the traditions of chivalry, knights and their quests, and the joys of imaginative narratives. His father, however, struggled with alcoholism and mental illness and, as a result, the family was far from wealthy.

At the age of nine, Doyle was sent to a Jesuit boarding school in England where he remained for several years. Upon graduation he entered the University of Edinburgh Medical School and during his time there also studied botany at the Royal Botanic Garden in Edinburgh. While studying, Doyle began writing short stories. During a medical externship in Birmingham, he wrote his first published piece, "The Mystery of Sasassa Valley," a story set in South Africa. It was printed in *Chambers's Edinburgh Journal* on September 6, 1879.

While in medical school, he met the exceptional man who became his mentor, Professor Dr. Joseph Bell, whose brilliant powers of observation followed by logical deduction Doyle later credited as the inspiration for Sherlock Holmes.

His first gainful employment as a doctor was as a medical officer on the steamship *Mayumba* as it travelled to the West African Coast. After that job, he set up a medical practice first in Plymouth, and then in Southsea, near Portsmouth. Over the next few years, he worked both as a doctor and a writer. In 1885, Doyle met and married his first wife, Louisa Hawkins. They moved to Montague Place near the British Museum and not far from Baker Street. They had a daughter and a son, Mary and Kingsley, but in 1893, Louisa contracted tuberculosis and suffered from it far many years.

In the spring of 1886, Doyle wrote a mystery novel, *A Tangled Skein*. He was not initially successful in getting it published, but in November of that year, with the name changed to *A Study in Scarlet,* it was accepted for publication in the 1887 *Beeton's Christmas Annual*. *A Study in Scarlet*, which introduced Sherlock Holmes and Dr. Watson, was not immediately popular. His second short novel, *The Sign of the Four,* likewise met with limited popularity. Beginning in the summer of 1891 his tales about the adventures of Sherlock Holmes began to appear in *The Strand Magazine* and then his popularity and that of Sherlock Holmes and Dr. Watson started to grow quickly in both Great Britain and the United States. Over the new four decades, Doyle would write sixty stories about Sherlock Holmes.

Having achieved fame and financial success as a writer, Doyle, at the age of thirty-two, quit medicine and devoted his time to writing. Throughout the later years of the nineteenth century and the first two decades of the twentieth, he wrote many other novels, short stories, histories, and essays. His most famous historical novel, *The White Company,* was published in 1891. Other fiction included a novel about the Napoleonic Era called *The Great Shadow,* published in 1892, and, in 1896, *Rodney Stone,* a story connected to the sport of boxing. His two-volume account of the Boer War, praising the British armed forces, led to his being knighted.

Although he wished to be recognized for his more serious literary writings, Doyle became and remains famous primarily for his stories about Sherlock Holmes. From the 1890s on he would write his most popular Sherlock Holmes books, including, *The Adventures of Sherlock Holmes* (1892), *The Memoirs of Sherlock Holmes*(1894) and *The Hound of the Baskervilles* (1901). All of these stories and most of his other short stories and essays originally appeared in *The Strand* magazine and were subsequently published in other magazines in the United States, and in book form as anthologies.

By 1893, Doyle wanted to rid himself of Sherlock Holmes so that he could concentrate his efforts on his other literary pursuits, especially writing more historical fiction. He killed off Holmes in the story *The Final Problem,* in which Holmes and the arch-villain Professor Moriarty fall to their death in the gorge of Reichenbach Falls in Switzerland.

The fans of Sherlock Holmes/Arthur Conan Doyle were disappointed and readership of *The Strand* plummeted. In 1901, Doyle reintroduced Sherlock Holmes in *The Hound of the Baskervilles,* setting the date of the story before Holmes's death. A few years later, after the period known to Sherlockians as *The Great Hiatus,* Doyle brought Sherlock Holmes back to life in *The Adventure of the Empty House.* He did so not in response to pressure from the reading public and his publishers, but primarily as a result of a exceptionally generous offer from the American magazine, *Collier's Weekly*.

In 1906, his wife Louisa finally succumbed to tuberculosis. The following year, he married again, this time to his longtime friend, Jean Leckie. They had three children – Denis, Adrian, and Jean - and they remained married until Doyle died.

During the final years of his life, Doyle travelled extensively on lecture tours to North America, Europe and the Antipodes, promoting Spiritualism. He continued to write about his religious convictions in a series of books, including

The New Revelation (1918), *The Vital Message*(1919), *The Wanderings of a Spiritualist* (1921) and *History of Spiritualism*(1926).

In 1928, Doyle's final twelve stories about Sherlock Holmes were published in a compilation entitled *The Case-Book of Sherlock Holmes*.

He continued his interest in and promotion of Spiritualism until his death, at age 71, in 1930. While some of his other writings, such as *The White Company,* and the *Professor Challenger* stories— especially the first in the series, *The Lost World*— continue to be enjoyed to this day by dedicated Sherlockians, Arthur Conan Doyle's undisputed gift to hundreds of millions of readers over the past century has been the stories and the character of Sherlock Holmes, the world's most famous detective.

Editor's Notes

By Craig Stephen Copland, Editor, and author of *The New Sherlock Holmes Mysteries.*

(www.SherlockHolmesMystery.com)

This story was published in October 1891, the sixth Sherlock Holmes story and the fourth of the increasingly popular shorter stories to be printed in *The Strand* magazine. In many ways it is an ideal gem of a Sherlock Holmes mystery. In his wonderful *Sherlock Holmes Handbook,* Chris Redmond states that it "may plausibly claim to be the perfect Sherlock Holmes story, offering everything readers have come to love, from a railway journey to a scene in which Holmes throws himself into the mud to look at clues through his lens. Once the mystery is solved and the innocent man cleared, to the discomfiture of Lestrade, Holmes arranges for the guilty man to go free, in view of extenuating circumstances."

There are several factors, themes and issues that I find significant when reading *The Boscombe Valley Mystery.*

It displays the classic Holmes methods: starting with general information, which may lead others to a hasty conclusion but upon which he retains an open mind; questioning of related people and adding data and insights; a close, forensic investigation of the crime site; interviewing of the accused; all the time assimilating all of the clues and data; rejecting the false conclusions of others; and finally being be led to the logically, inevitable correct conclusion. The reader is with Holmes all of the way and we see the short-sightedness of Lestrade (and to a lesser extent,

Watson), and the innocence of James, as testified to by the woman in love with him.

Underlying this progression is an examination of what constitutes *evidence.* In the train, during his conversation with Watson, Holmes pronounces on the unreliability of "circumstantial evidence" which can be "a very tricky thing." Had James McCarthy been tried only on the circumstantial evidence, he would have been hung. Fortunately, Holmes was wise enough to see beyond the obvious.

Parallel to the issue of evidence is that of *justice*. Holmes, inexplicably, allows a man who has admitted to murder and robbery in his past, and to the murder of his neighbor, to go free. The fact that the man did not have long to live because of his diabetes, does not excuse this travesty.

Yet justice, of another sort, does triumph. There is a obvious recognition of "be sure your sins will find you out." John Turner paid, in a way, for the sins of his past by the twenty years of torment that McCarthy visited upon him. Outwardly, he appears to lead a comfortable life but his wife dies early and he is beset with crippling diabetes. Universal law prevails and crimes do not go unpunished.

One of the very interesting aspects of this story is its revelation of the knowledge of and attitudes toward Australia by Victorians. Although only a relatively small percentage of the settlers of Australia were the convicts who first were sent to Botany Bay, they accounted for a major part of the image that was held of the territory. If Australia were to be judged by the accounts in this story, it would be perceived as a rough, lawless place inhabited by get-rich-quick gold miners, highwaymen, and murderers who gave decent Englishmen a reason to distrust them should they return to England. Actually, it had a far more complex history and social structure, as was made evident in the great history of the country, *The Fatal Shore,* by Robert Hughes. But in 1891, that was not they way Londoners thought about it.

Sherlock Holmes in Large Print

The following stories will soon be available in large print and in Aphont.

- A Study in Scarlet
- The Sign of the Four
- The Hound of the Baskervilles
- The Valley of fear
- A Scandal in Bohemia
- The Red-Headed League
- A Case of Identity
- The Boscombe Valley Mystery
- The Five Orange Pips
- The Man with the Twisted Lip
- The Blue Carbuncle
- The Speckled Band
- The Engineer's Thumb
- The Noble Bachelor

The Beryl Coronet

The Copper Beeches

Silver Blaze

The Yellow Face

The Stock-Broker's Clerk

The "Gloria Scott"

The Musgrave Ritual

The Reigate Puzzle

The Crooked Man

The Resident Patient

The Greek Interpreter

The Naval Treaty

The Final Problem

The Empty House

The Norwood Builder

The Dancing Men

The Solitary Cyclist

The Priory School

Black Peter

Charles Augustus Milverton

The Six Napoleons

The Three Students

The Golden Pince-Nez

The Missing Three-Quarter

The Abbey Grange

The Second Stain

The Cardboard Box

Wisteria Lodge

The Bruce-Partington Plans

The Devil's Foot

The Red Circle

The Disappearance of Lady Frances Carfax

The Dying Detective

His Last Bow

About the Series Editor

Elementary, my dear reader. What else, after fifty years of enjoying the stories of Sherlock Holmes, is a recently retired gentleman to do with his time but write more stories about the world's most beloved detective.

Craig Stephen Copland confesses that he discovered Sherlock Holmes when, some time in the muddled early 1960s he pinched his older brother's copy of the immortal stories and was forever afterward thoroughly hooked. He is very grateful to his high school English teachers in Toronto who inculcated in him a love of literature and writing, and even inspired him to be an English major at the University of Toronto. There he was blessed to sit at the feet of both Northrup Frye and Marshall McLuhan, and other great literary professors, who led him to believe that he was called to be a high school English teacher.

It was his good fortune to come to his pecuniary senses and abandoned that goal and pursued a varied professional career that took him to over one hundred countries and endless adventures. He considers himself to have been and to continue to be one of the luckiest men on God's good earth.

A few years back he took a step in the direction of Sherlockian studies and joined the Sherlock

Holmes Society of Canada—also known as the Toronto Bootmakers. In May of 2014 this esteemed group of scholars announced a contest for the writing of a new Sherlock Holmes mystery. Although he had never tried his hand at fiction before, Craig entered and was pleasantly surprised to be selected as one of the winners. Having enjoyed the experience he decided to write more of the same, and is now on a mission to write a new Sherlock Holmes mystery that is related to and inspired by each of the sixty stories in the original Canon.

If you are interested in reading yet more Sherlock Holmes pastiche mysteries, you should checkout Craig's website:

www.SherlockHolmesMystery.com

All of the stories are set in Victorian/Edwardian London – with a few trips to other locations – and revolve around the traditional characters of

Holmes and Watson, as well as the characters in the original story. But then a whole new mystery is unveiled. The New Sherlock Holmes Mysteries s are available in large print, and fonts and formats designed for those who are visually impaired. They are available from online retailers in most countries:

For personal and family reasons Craig became concerned about the lack of a Large Print format of the Canon that made use of the latest best practices in special fonts and recommended colors and layouts for the visually impaired and the elderly. As a result he undertook to re-published all of the Sherlock Holmes stories in this new Large Print series.

He currently lives and writes in Toronto, New York, the Okanagan Valley, and Tokyo, and looks forward to finally settling down when he turns ninety.

CPSIA information can be obtained
at www.ICGtesting.com
Printed in the USA
LVOW09s0252200217
524791LV00010B/263/P

9 781535 551571